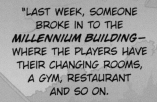

"LAST WEEK, SOMEONE BROKE IN TO THE *MILLENNIUM BUILDING*—WHERE THE PLAYERS HAVE THEIR CHANGING ROOMS, A GYM, RESTAURANT AND SO ON.

"THE INTRUDER *DISABLED* THE CCTV CAMERAS AND THE ALARM. A THOROUGHLY *PROFESSIONAL* JOB. WE ONLY KNOW HE WAS THERE AT *ALL* BECAUSE A SECURITY GUARD SAW HIM *LEAVING*.

"HE WAS A YOUNG CHINESE MAN, DRESSED ALL IN BLACK AND WEARING A *RUCKSACK*.

YOU SAID HE WAS A *PROFESSIONAL*. WHY IS THAT SO *STRANGE?*

"THE *POLICE* SEARCHED THE WHOLE CLUB WITH SNIFFER DOGS. THE ANTI-TERRORIST SQUAD WAS THERE FOR *THREE DAYS*. BUT THEY FOUND *NOTHING*. WHOEVER IT WAS JUST *VANISHED.*"

IT ISN'T. BUT HE DIDN'T *TAKE* ANYTHING, EITHER! NOT A *SAUSAGE!*

MAYBE THE GUARD *DISTURBED* HIM BEFORE HE COULD GET HIS HANDS ON WHATEVER IT WAS HE WAS *AFTER.*

NO, HE WAS ALREADY *LEAVING* WHEN HE WAS SEEN.

NOW, ISN'T *THAT* STRANGE?

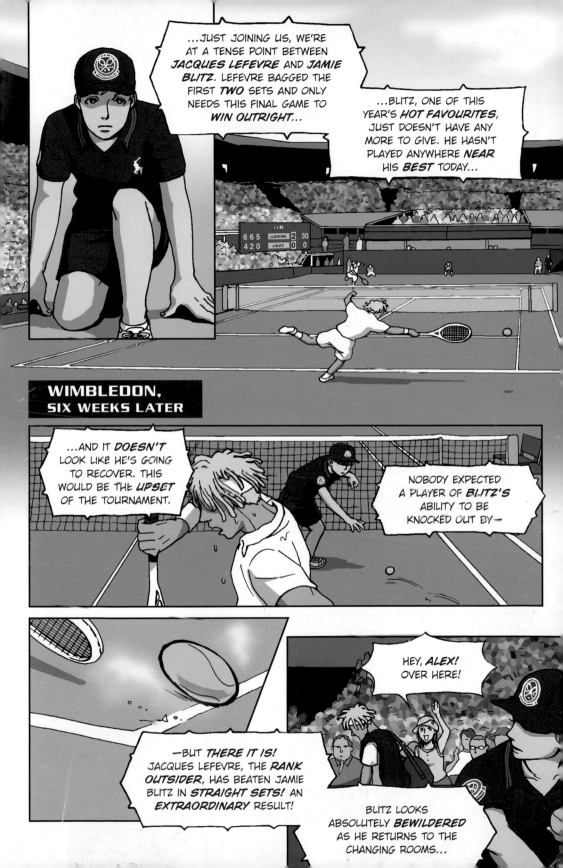

SKELETON KEY
ANTHONY HOROWITZ

Adapted by Antony Johnston

Illustrated by
Kanako Damerum & Yuzuru Takasaki

WALKER
BOOKS

YOU COULD HAVE GOT YOURSELF *KILLED*. I DON'T LIKE MY AGENTS TAKING *UNNECESSARY RISKS*.

I'M *NOT* ONE OF YOUR AGENTS.

CRAWFORD HAD *NO RIGHT* TO INVOLVE YOU IN THIS BUSINESS.

LIVERPOOL STREET, LONDON

THERE'S ENOUGH *DANGER* IN OFFICIAL MISSIONS WITHOUT *ADDING* TO IT. TAKING ON A *TRIAD* SINGLE-HANDED!

IT WAS JUST *ONE MAN*.

BUT THAT MAN IS PART OF A *HUGE* ORGANIZATION. *BIG CIRCLE* IS A RELATIVELY NEW TRIAD, BUT IT'S ALSO ONE OF THE MOST *VIOLENT*.

THEY DON'T TAKE KINDLY TO PEOPLE *INTERFERING* WITH THEIR BUSINESS.

THANKS FOR THE *LECTURE*. I'LL BEAR IT IN MIND.

SIT *DOWN*, ALEX. YOU HAVE *NO IDEA* WHAT YOU'VE GOT YOURSELF INTO.

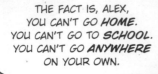

THE FACT IS, ALEX, YOU CAN'T GO *HOME*. YOU CAN'T GO TO *SCHOOL*. YOU CAN'T GO *ANYWHERE* ON YOUR OWN.

WE'VE ALREADY ARRANGED FOR *JACK STARBRIGHT* TO BE SENT *OUT* OF LONDON. WE CAN'T TAKE *ANY* CHANCES.

SO WHAT AM I MEANT TO *DO?*

WELL...

BY *COINCIDENCE*, WE HAD A REQUEST FOR YOUR SERVICES A FEW DAYS AGO.

THE AMERICAN *CIA* NEEDS A YOUNG PERSON FOR AN *OPERATION* THEY'RE MOUNTING.

YOU'VE ALWAYS TOLD ME TO KEEP EVERYTHING *SECRET*, BUT ALL THIS TIME YOU'VE BEEN *BRAGGING* ABOUT ME?!

ABSOLUTELY *NOT*.

BUT THINGS HAVE A WAY OF...

LEAKING...

IN OUR LINE OF WORK.

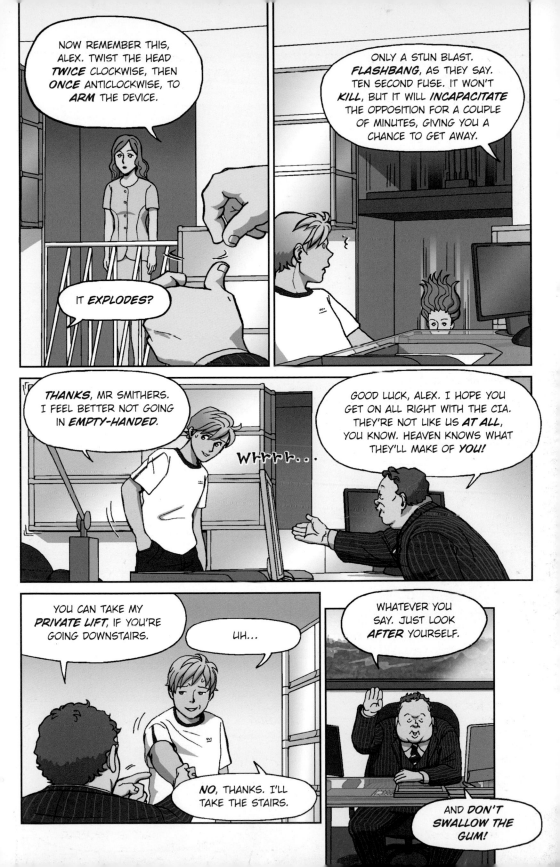

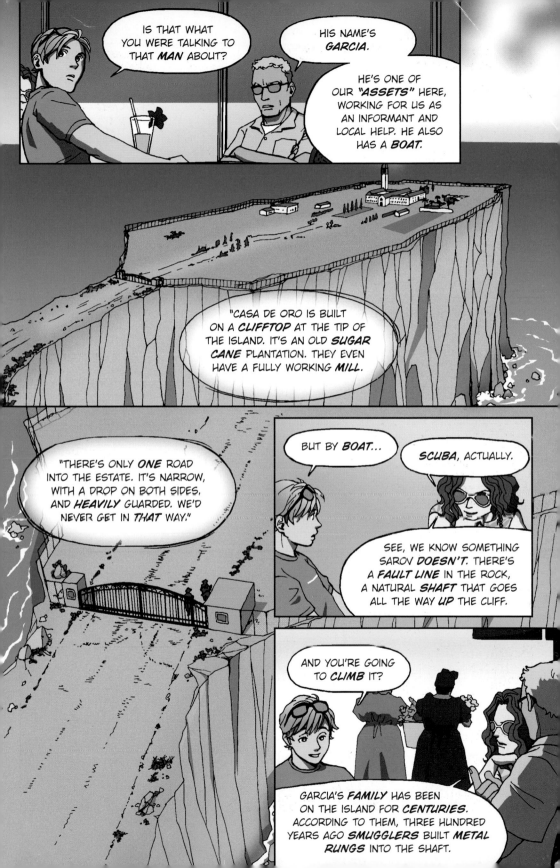

IT'S *TURNING* TO ATTACK AGAIN. ONLY GOT *ONE CHANCE*...

S+ab!

Nnngh!

BARELY A *SCRATCH*. AND NOW IT'S COMING *BACK!*

GOT TO GET IN THE CAVE, GET *OUT* OF THE WATER...

...TOO LATE!

I WILL **UNDO** THE DAMAGE OF THE LAST THIRTY YEARS! I WILL **GIVE** MY COUNTRY BACK ITS **PRIDE** AND POSITION ON THE **WORLD STAGE!**

I AM NOT AN **EVIL** MAN, ALEX.

WHATEVER YOUR SUPERIORS **TOLD** YOU, MY **ONLY** WISH IS TO STOP THIS **DISEASE** AND MAKE THE WORLD A **BETTER PLACE.**

I HOPE YOU CAN **BELIEVE** THAT. IT MATTERS **VERY MUCH** TO ME THAT YOU SHOULD COME TO SEE THINGS **MY** WAY.

WE WILL **BREAKFAST** TOGETHER AT NINE A.M., THEN I WILL SHOW YOU THE **ESTATE.**

DO NOT TRY TO **ESCAPE.** THERE IS NO WAY **DOWN** TO THE COURTYARD, AND THIS DOOR WILL BE **LOCKED.**

THIS WAS ONCE A SUGAR FARM, WORKED BY *SLAVES*. THERE WERE ALMOST A *MILLION* SLAVES IN CUBA AND CAYO ESQUELETO.

AT *FOUR-THIRTY* EVERY MORNING THEY WOULD RING A *BELL* UP THERE, FOR THE SLAVES TO START WORK. THEY ALL CAME FROM *WEST AFRICA*.

THEY WORKED HERE... AND THEY *DIED* HERE.

THAT BUILDING IS THE *BARRACÓN*, THE *HOUSE OF SLAVES*. TWO HUNDRED OF THEM SLEPT IN THERE, PENNED IN LIKE *ANIMALS*.

IF WE HAVE TIME, I WILL SHOW YOU THE *PUNISHMENT* BLOCK. CAN YOU *IMAGINE* BEING FASTENED BY YOUR ANKLES FOR *WEEKS*, UNABLE TO MOVE, *STARVING* AND *THIRSTY*?

I DON'T *WANT* TO IMAGINE IT.

OF *COURSE* NOT. THE WESTERN WORLD PREFERS TO *FORGET* THE CRIMES THAT MADE IT *RICH*.

YAAA!

HE *KILLED* TURNER AND TROY WITHOUT A *THOUGHT*... BUT HE WANTS ME *ALIVE*.

WHY?

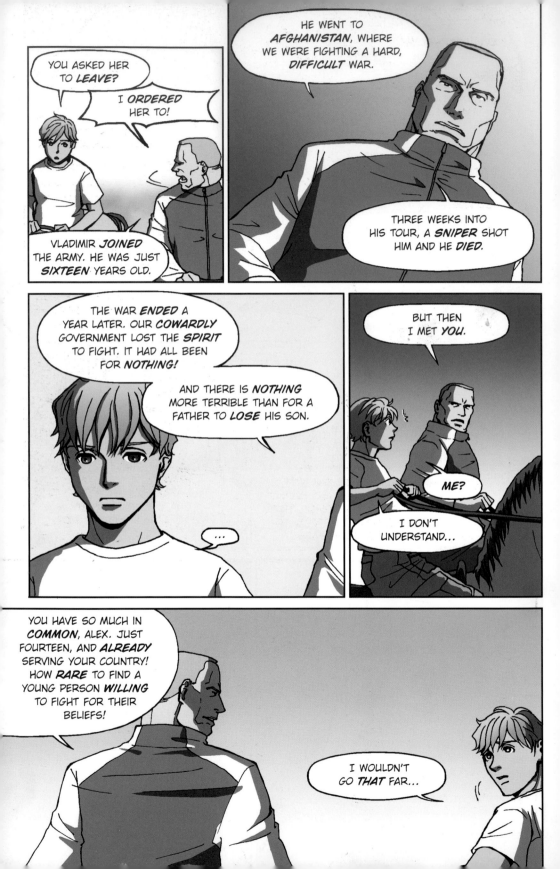

LISTEN TO THE SOUND OF YOUR OWN *FEAR!* IT *BETRAYS* YOU!

DUMDUMDUMDU

BHANNG.

AND WHEN YOU HEAR *SILENCE* - IT COULD BE ANY MOMENT, NOW - *THAT* IS WHEN YOU WILL KNOW YOU ARE *DEAD.*

HE HAS *LEARNED* HIS LESSON.

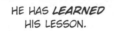

CUBA
HDA 0147

TAKE HIM BACK TO HIS *ROOM.*

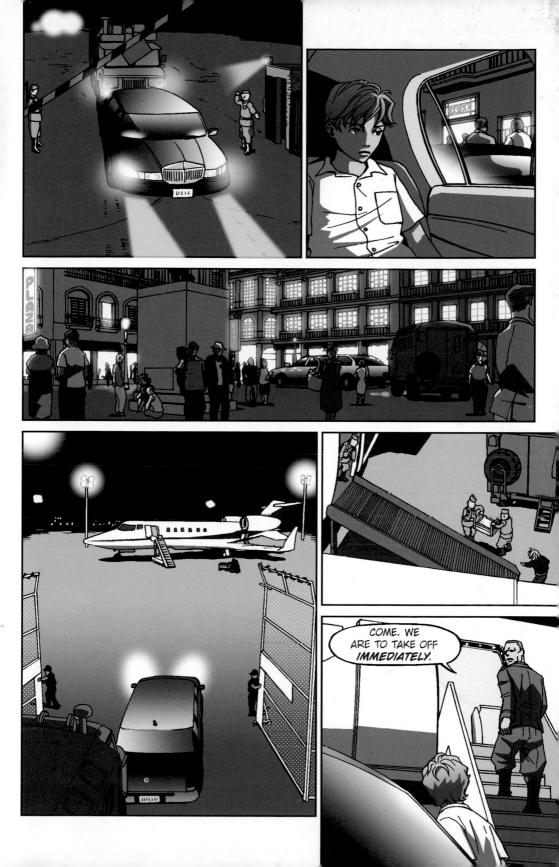

COME. WE ARE TO TAKE OFF *IMMEDIATELY.*

WE'VE *LOST* ALEX RIDER.

SORRY, ALAN. I KNOW IT'S *NOT* WHAT YOU WANTED TO HEAR, BUT THAT'S THE *END* OF IT.

MMM.

HE DID VERY *WELL*.

IT WOULDN'T *SURPRISE* ME IF THE CIA STARTED TRAINING THEIR *OWN* TEENAGE SPY NOW. THEY'RE *ALWAYS* COPYING OUR IDEAS.

WHEN *WE'RE* NOT COPYING *THEIRS*.

OH, YES. I HAD AN EMAIL FROM *JOE BYRNE* AT THE *CIA*. HE WAS UPSET ABOUT THE LOSS OF HIS *OWN* AGENTS, BUT HE WAS FULL OF *PRAISE* FOR ALEX.

HE DEFINITELY OWES US A *FAVOUR*.

I'VE READ THE *FILE*, BUT PERHAPS YOU CAN FILL ME IN ON THE *DETAILS*. HOW *EXACTLY* DID THE RUSSIANS FIND OUT ABOUT SAROV IN *TIME*?

BECAUSE OF WHAT HAPPENED AT *EDINBURGH AIRPORT.* ALEX *ESCAPED* FROM SAROV'S PLANE AND RAN INTO A *SECURITY GUARD.*

ALEX ACTUALLY TOLD HIM THE *TRUTH* ABOUT HIMSELF, ABOUT US, *EVERYTHING.* BUT THE GUARD DIDN'T *BELIEVE* IT.

"SAROV CAUGHT UP WITH THEM AND *SHOT* THE GUARD. ALEX MUST HAVE THOUGHT THAT WAS THE *END* OF IT...

"...BUT *LUCKILY* FOR US, THE GUARD'S *RADIO* WAS ACTIVATED THE WHOLE TIME. HIS OFFICE HEARD *EVERYTHING.*"

THEY DIDN'T BELIEVE IT *EITHER,* OF COURSE... UNTIL THEY FOUND HIM WITH A *BULLET* IN HIS HEAD. THEN THEY CALLED *US.*

I CONTACTED MURMANSK, AND THE RUSSIANS *STORMED* THE YARD WITH A NAVAL FORCE AND GUNSHIPS.

WHAT HAPPENED TO THE *NUCLEAR BOMB?*

DON'T YOUR PARENTS MIND?
THEY LIKE YOU, ALEX. WE'RE JUST GOING TO BORROW A FRIEND'S HOUSE, IT'S NOTHING FANCY.
WELL, APART FROM THE SWIMMING POOL. AND THE MARINA. AND THE STABLES...
A REAL FAMILY HOLIDAY...
YOU DO LOOK LIKE YOU NEED A REST, ALEX. COME WITH US AND GET AWAY FROM ALL... THIS.
THAT'S THE BEST IDEA I'VE HEARD IN WEEKS.
COME ON, LET'S GET SOMETHING TO EAT. I'M STARVING.
THE END

First published 2009 by Walker Books Ltd
87 Vauxhall Walk, London SE11 5HJ

2 4 6 8 10 9 7 5 3 1

Text and illustrations © 2009 Walker Books Ltd
Based on the original novel *Skeleton Key* © 2002 Anthony Horowitz

Anthony Horowitz has asserted his moral rights.

Trademarks 2009 Stormbreaker Productions Ltd
Alex Rider™, Boy with torch Logo™, AR Logo™

This book has been typeset in Wild Words and Serpentine Bold

Printed in Italy

British Library Cataloguing in Publication Data:
a catalogue record for this book is available
from the British Library

ISBN 978-1-4063-1348-2

www.walker.co.uk

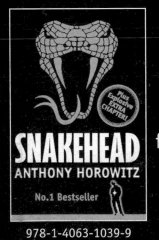

☢ ANTHONY HOROWITZ (BA/Nielsen Author of the Year 2007) is one of the most popular children's writers working today. His hugely successful Alex Rider series has sold over ten million copies worldwide and won numerous awards, including the Children's Book of the Year Award for ARK ANGEL at the 2006 British Book Awards and the Red House Children's Book Award for SKELETON KEY. He scripted the blockbuster movie STORMBREAKER from his own novel, and also writes extensively for TV, with programmes including MIDSOMER MURDERS, POIROT and FOYLE'S WAR. He is married to television producer Jill Green and lives in London with his two sons, Nicholas and Cassian, and their dog, Loser.

www.anthonyhorowitz.com

☢ ANTONY JOHNSTON, who wrote the script for this book, has written more than fifteen other graphic novels, including WOLVERINE: PRODIGAL SON, THE LONG HAUL and THREE DAYS IN EUROPE. He also writes a monthly comic series, WASTELAND, and has written more miniseries and short stories than he can remember. In addition to his comics work he writes novels, such as FRIGHTENING CURVES (which won the 2002 IPPY award for Best Horror) and STEALING LIFE, and has also written videogames, such as 2008's DEAD SPACE. Antony lives in north-west England with his partner Marcia, his dogs Connor and Rosie, and far too many Macs and iPods.

www.antonyjohnston.com

☢ The artwork in this graphic novel is the work of two artists, **KANAKO DAMERUM** and **YUZURU TAKASAKI,** who collaborate on every illustration. Although living on opposite sides of the globe, these Japanese sisters work seamlessly together via the Internet.

Living and working in Tokyo, **YUZURU** produced all the line work for these illustrations using traditional means. The quality of her draughtsmanship comes from years of honing her skills in the highly competitive world of manga.

KANAKO lives and works out of her studio in London. She managed and directed the project as well as colouring and rendering the artwork digitally using her wealth of knowledge in graphic design.

www.manga-media.com
www.thorogood.net